DIARY

OF A
MINECRAFT
ZOMBIE

Book 14

by Zack Zombie

Monday

"I'm not fat! I'm just chubby, that's all."

"Yeah, right. You're so fat that you stepped on a scale and it said, 'To Be Continued'!"

"HAHAHAHA!"

"Stop it! That's not funny," Slimey said as tears started welling up in his eyes.

"You're so fat, you brought a spoon to the Super Bowl!" Darius the Enderman said.

"HAHAHAHA!"

Oh, man. I could tell Slimey was about to break. And Darius and his friends weren't letting up.

"You're so fat, not even Dora can explore you!"

1

"HAHAHAHA!"

"WAAAAAAAAAAHHHHHH!!!!!"

Yup. That's it. Slimey's done.

After obliterating all of Slimey's self-esteem, I thought it was over.

But Darius and his group of minions weren't finished yet. Then they set their sights on Creepy.

"You're so dumb, you thought a quarterback was a refund!" Quentin said.

"HAHAHAHA!"

"Yeah, you're so dumb, you went to the dentist to get a Bluetooth!" Chad said.

"HAHAHAHA!"

"Naw, you're so dumb, when somebody said it was chilly outside, you grabbed a bowl!" Darius said.

"HAHAHAHA!"

WAAAAAHHHHHH!!!!!

HSSSSSSSSSS!!!!

Then Darius and his friends ran away before Creepy went nuclear.

But, me and the guys helped Creepy calm down.

"That was close," I said.

"Why. . .sniff. . .are. . .sniff. . .those. . . sniff. . . guys. . .sniff. . .so. . .sniff. . .mean? WAAAAAAAHHH!!" Creepy asked between sobs.

"I don't know, Creepy. . .I don't know."

Actually, I did know.

I think Darius took a blood oath to be my mortal enemy for life.

But I don't get what the big deal is.

I mean, all I did was beat him at the National Minecraft PVP championship.

And, yeah, maybe me and Ellie did rat on him for cheating.

. . .which got him banned for life from every Minecraft server on the planet.

. . .And which made him lose all his Gaming sponsorships.

. . .And which got him put on academic probation at school.

. . .And which made him the laughing stock in our whole town. . . as well as the other 12 biomes.

But I still don't get what the big deal is.

But ever since then, Darius and his minions have been terrorizing me and the guys for weeks.

The worst part is that it's happening right when we're all going through puberty.

Which is like free ammo for Darius and his goons.

I mean like, I already feel dumb that both of my legs are the same size, which is really weird for a zombie.

And I already feel weird that I have hair growing out of my ears. . .or where my ears would be if I had any.

And I feel really weird that I occasional smell like. . .uh. . .you know. . .minty fresh.

Sniff. . .BLECH!

But the other guys got it real bad.

Like, Slimey is so fat that he only wears parachute pants now. And when I mean pants, I mean a parachute with a rope on it.

And Creepy's head is like two sizes too big.

I mean, his head is so big, he doesn't have dreams anymore. He has movies.

I think somebody even said his head is so big it shows up on radar.

Though, the good thing is that when it rains, his feet never get wet.

And Skelly got it bad too.

Right now, he's so skinny, that he has to run around in the shower just to get wet.

He even said he can do a hula hoop with a Cheerio.

Man, just when I thought I was on top of the world.

I mean, I really thought I was going to be popular this year.

Like, I was going to be the king of the hill.

Now, I'm more like the king of the pimple.

Figures.

Tuesday

I was looking in the mirror today, and I noticed a lot of other things that've been happening to me since going through puberty.

Like, I started noticing some dirt where my upper lip would be.

I was thinking about shaving it, but I couldn't find a razor for my teeth.

Also, I found these really big pimples growing on my back.

They kinda made me look a little like Quasimodo.

I tried to touch my pimples to see what they felt like.

But then they popped.

Now, I just look like I took a bath in cottage cheese.

"Zombie, are you still staring at yourself in front of the mirror?" my mom asked. "You've been there for over an hour."

"YETH, MASTHER!"

"Uh, Zombie, are you all right?"

"YETH, MASTHER!"

"OK, well, dinner's almost ready."

"YETH, MASTHER!"

My mom walked out of my room with a weird look on her face.

But, I'm just glad that she left.

I started getting really tired of holding my Science book.

You know. . .

To cover my bony knees.

Wednesday

I went to go see Steve today.

I wonder if Steve has to worry about stuff like puberty.

I mean, ever since I've known him he always kinda looked the same.

But, who knows, maybe Steve had a round head before.

And instead of punching trees, maybe he used to punch something else.

Like Zombies. . .gulp!

Naw, what am I thinking. Steve would never hurt a Zombie. . .Right?

"Hey, Steve."

"Yo, Zombie, what's crackalackin'?"

"Well, actually, since you asked. . ."

"POP!"

"Ewww! Dude, doesn't that hurt?"

"Naw, not really. Plus, it comes in really handy when we play baseball."

"POP!"

"There you go, good as new."

"Bro, warn a guy before you do that," Steve said. "So nasty."

"Anyway, Steve, I got a question for you."

"Yeah, what's up?"

"Hey, did you ever like, you know. . .um. . .go through. . .changes?"

"What kinda changes?" Steve asked.

"Uh. . .you know. . .changes. . . like when your body starts to grow stuff, and uh. . .do stuff and like fall off and stuff. . ."

Steve just gave me his usual confused look.

"Oh, you mean like puberty?"

"Yeah, yeah. . .puberty, yeah. . ."

"Yup. Sure did. Like, I don't know if you know this, but I was a really chubby kid when I was younger," Steve said. "Here's a picture."

"Seriously?"

"Yeah. I didn't always have this strong chiseled body, you know. It took years of training to get it this way."

I just started at Steve, confused.

"So, you actually wanted to look like that?"

"Ha, ha. Funny. I also didn't always punch trees you know," Steve continued. "I used to punch Zom. . ."

RRRRUUUUMMMMBBBBLLLLEEEE!!!!!

All of a sudden, there was a huge earthquake around Steve's house.

"What the what was that?!!!"

"Oh, that's just the underground volcano," Steve said. "It always does that around this time of year."

"What underground volcano?"

"You know, in the Nether," Steve said. "Though, it's kinda weird. It's never been this strong before."

"Hey, I used to play hide and seek in the Nether with my cousin Piggy. But I never saw any volcano."

"Yeah, it's behind the old Nether Fortress. It's been pretty quiet for like 600,000 years. But it sometimes passes gas once in a while, which sometimes causes the ground to rumble."

"Whoa, a Nether fart. So cool."

When I left Steve, I was really happy to hear that Minecraft mobs weren't the only ones that go through changes.

Humans do too.

And, volcanos can fart.

So cool.

But, you know, Steve didn't let his chubbiness keep him down.

Instead, he made himself the man he is today.

Yeah, he looks weird. . . especially with his incredibly big square head.

But if Steve can do it, I can too.

As a matter of fact, you know what?

This year, I'm not just going to be popular. . .

I'm going to be the most popular kid in school!

And neither Darius, nor his minions are going to stop me.

And as for puberty, ha!

I laugh at you! HA! HA! HA! HA!

You know, for all I know, puberty probably doesn't even exist.

Thursday

At lunchtime today, I went to the library to get some ideas on how to be more popular.

CLICKETY CLACK, CLICKETY CLACK, CLICKETY CLACK.

I'm sure there's something on the Ender-net about how to be more popular.

CLICKETY CLACK, CLICKETY CLACK, CLICKETY CLACK.

Yeah, here's a good article.

'HOW TO BE A POPULAR ZOMBIE IN 3 EASY STEPS'

Nice, I like easy.

Let see. . .Number 1—Get Noticed.

OK. Now how do I do that?

It's all about confidence. Zombie Confidence has a lot to do with body language. Walk with your head really low and your arms at your sides while dragging your knuckles on the floor. Also, make sure to hunch and walk with a limp. Remember, the bigger the limp the bigger the crowd you'll attract.

Hmmm. . .that one's gonna be a little tough. Especially the limping part. Yeah, that's been really hard since my legs recently grew the same size.

Puberty…

So wrong.

All right, let's see what else it says. . .

To get noticed in class, raise your hand, and answer every question the teacher asks. And never be afraid to speak up!

20

OK, that's a little better. I can do that. ·

As a matter of fact, I'm going to try it in my next class.

Man, at this rate, I'll be the most popular kid in school by the end of the week.

Sigh. Good times.

Thursday – Later that day. . .

"**A**ll right, boys and girls. Who can recite the Minecraft National Anthem for us?" Ms. Bones asked.

Darius and his minions started snickering and pointing fingers at any kid who thought about raising their hand.

But, I knew this was my chance to really get noticed.

"I can, Ms. Bones," I said.

"All right, Zombie, please start."

Well here it goes. . .

"Boomdiyadda, Boomdiyadda, Boomdiyadda, Boomdiyadda. . .

I love the mountains.

I love the clear blue skies.

I love big bridges.

I love when wolves run by.

I love the whole world.

And all explosive sounds.

Boomdiyadda, Boomdiyadda, Boomdiyadda, Boomdiyadda. . .

I love some redstone.

I love my zombie friends.

I love hot laba. . .

I mean Hob lava. . .Hob laba. . .

I lub hob laba. . .

Hob laba. . ."

"LOOK!" somebody yelled.

All of a sudden, I looked down and I noticed these two big pieces of zombie flesh hanging off of my face.

"ZOMBIE'S GOT LIPS!" somebody else yelled.

"HAHAHAHA!"

Then all the kid started laughing at me.

"Hey, Zombie, your lips are so big that whenever you smile, you get Chapstick in your ears!" Darius said.

"HAHAHAHA!"

"Hey, Zombie, your lips are so big, you can smile and wash your hair at the same time!" Quentin said.

"HAHAHAHA!"

"Hey, Zombie, your lips are so big that Chapstick had to invent a spray!" Chad said.

"HAHAHAHA!"

I tried to run out of the classroom, but my lips were so big that I tripped over them on my way out the door.

"HAHAHAHA!"

After tripping a few more times, I finally made it to the janitor's closet and locked myself in.

Then, after a little while, I heard a knocking at the door.

"Hey, Zombie, you in there?"

"Creeby, is bab you?"

"Yeah, Skelly and Slimey are here too. Are you OK?"

"WAAAAAAAABABABABAHHHH! "Wabs habbening to me?"

"I don't know, man, but we can sneak you out," Creepy said. "But you need to hurry cause Darius and a whole crowd of kids are coming this way."

So I opened the door.

The guys tried to put a jacket over my head to hide me as we snuck out. But I kept tripping over my lips.

"I got an idea!" Skelly said.

Then everything went black.

All I heard was a lot of muffled laughter until we got outside.

Then I could see again.

"Man, your new lips make a great hoody," Skelly said.

"WAAAAAAAABABABABAHHHH!"

I finally got to my house.

I wanted to go straight to my room and jump into bed and pretend this wasn't happening to me, but…

FRBLNKT!

FRBLFFT!

FRBLMPT!

I just kept tripping on my lips going up the stairs to my room.

Finally, I just threw my lips over my shoulder and went upstairs.

I opened the door and jumped into bed. And I just laid there in bed, miserable.

Since I didn't know what else to do, I just put my new lips over my head and cried myself to sleep.

Friday

"**B**ub, Momb, I can't go boo school loobing like bis!"

"Oh, Zombie, stop being so dramatic," my mom said. "You're just going through puberty, that's all. And to be honest, it kind of looks cute on you."

"Son, this is natural. All Zombies go through mutations during puberty," my dad said.

"WAB?!!!"

"Yes, son. When I went through puberty, my ears grew really, really big. I was really sad until I realized that I could fly to places a whole lot faster. They came in really handy when I was late for school."

"WAAAAAAAABABABABAHHHH!"

"Come on, Zombie, off you go," my mom said. "School is going to start soon, and you don't want to be late."

Then my mom took my lips and wrapped them around my neck a few times.

She said they would keep me warm, but I knew what she was doing.

And it wasn't working.

I started walking down the street, and when I got around the corner I decided to ditch my first few classes at school.

I know I wasn't supposed to, but I couldn't go to school looking like this.

So, I went to the only person that I knew who could help me.

"Hey, Steeb."

"Whoa! Zombie, you look like you got your head stuck in a Minecart. What happened?"

"Puberby."

"Seriously? Man, and I thought humans had it bad."

"WAAAAAAAABABABABAHHHH! Can you helb me?"

"Uh. . .yeah, I think I have a shrink potion that can clear that up," Steve said. "I'll go get it."

Ugh! Finally, some good news in my life.

I knew it. If anybody could help me get out of this jam, it was Steve.

"Here you go, Zombie," he said, handing a potion bottle to me. "But it's really strong, so only take a few drops, OK?"

"Oh-bay."

Then I ran to school just in time for my next class.

I snuck over to the janitor's closet and unwrapped my lip scarf so I could take the potion. Then I reached over to put a few drops of the potion in my mouth.

But as I was reaching for it, I tripped again.

THUMPT!

SPLASH!

Lucky for me, the potion landed on my bottom lip. . .

Friday – Later that day. . .

"**H**AHAHAHA!"

"Zombie, you're so short, you need a step stool just to get on a step stool!" Quentin said.

"HAHAHAHA!"

"Zombie, you're so short, you broke your leg jumping off the toilet!" Chad said.

"HAHAHAHA!"

"Zombie, you're so short, when you sneezed you bumped your head on the floor!" Darius said.

"HAHAHAHA!"

Then I found myself in the janitor's closet again.

Yeah, things didn't go as expected.

The good news is that my big lips are gone.

The bad news is that right now I'm so small I didn't even have to open the door to the janitor's closet to get in.

And when I mean small, I mean like, I can use a sock for a sleeping bag kinda small.

Or like, I can do limbo under the door kinda small.

Or like, I can play handball on the curb kinda small.

So much for my plan to be more popular.

Man, I'm already below average on the popularity scale.

And right now, I just dropped down to the same category as boogers, toe jam and belly button hair.

Though, I don't know why those are unpopular. . .they're actually pretty tasty.

Anyway, what am I going to do now?

There's no hope for me.

I'm doomed.

Saturday

So, I woke up this morning and I was back to normal.

It seems that the effects of Steve's potion were only temporary.

But, man, that was rough.

It's like, no matter how hard I try, something is always trying to hold me down.

GRRRRRRRRRR!

What was that?

Then, I felt something weird under my shirt.

So I lifted up my shirt, and my stomach started to bubble.

All of a sudden. . .

POP!

"WHAT THE WHAT!"

Next thing I know, there's a huge round piece of zombie flesh where my bellybutton used to be.

"WAAAAAAAAAAAAAAAHHHH!"

Man, I thought my outie was big before. . .Now its huge!

"WAAAAAAAAAAAAAAAHHHH!"

"Zombie, what in the world is the matter?" my mom asked, running into my room.

"Mom. . .LOOK!" I said as I lifted my shirt.

"WAAAAAAAAAAAAAAAHHHH!"

37

"Oh, Zombie, it's not that bad. Your father has one, and I think it's really cute," she said.

"WAAAAAAAAAAAAAAHHHH!"

"We even named it," she said. "We call it Zack."

"WAAAAAAAAAAAAAAAHHHH!"

Oh, man, and I thought things couldn't get any worse.

But then I could swear that I saw my outie wink at me.

Saturday – Later that Day

It's a good thing my outie went back to normal size.

I would hate to have to live the rest of my life with that thing.

I mean, it's hard enough to keep one mouth fed on this body.

But don't get me wrong, it did start to grow on me.

No seriously, it kept growing until it was the size of a head.

And it had hair, and eyes and everything.

I decided to call him Justin.

I could even make him move if I flexed my muscles.

But the singing eventually got on my nerves, so I knew he had to go.

Sunday

Today, I decided to go see Steve and take my mind off my troubles.

"Hey, Steve."

"Hey, Zomb. . .Whoa!"

"Whoa to you too. What's up?"

"Uh. . .Zombie."

"Yeah, Steve?"

"Um. . .you OK there, buddy?"

"Yeah. Why do you ask?"

"Uh. . .you look like you just came back from a Zombie Villager convention."

"What do you mean?" I asked, a little scared to get the answer.

"Here, take a look," Steve said as he handed me a mirror. "Nice unibrow, though."

And there it was. A huge, bulbous piece of Zombie meat stuck right on my face.

"HWAAAAAAAAAAAAAAAHHHH! What's happening to me?"

"It's OK, man," Steve said. "Having a nose is cool."

43

"Sniff. . .really?"

"Yeah, it's like having an extra chin but on your forehead."

"HWAAAAAAAAAAAAAAAHHHH!"

Then I ran all the way back home.

Suddenly, I ran into Old Man Jenkins on the way home.

"Hey, Mr. Jenkins."

"Whoa, Zombie. Looks like you're going through some changes, huh?"

"How'd you guess?"

"Oh, I don't know. . .it's as plain as the nose on your face, ha ha!"

"Sniff. . .sniff. . .HWAAAAAAAAAAAAHHHH!"

"Oh, I'm sorry, Zombie. Didn't mean to curdle your milk. I was just trying to cheer you up a bit."

"Mr. Jenkins, what am I gonna do? No matter how hard I try, I can't stop from mutating."

"I remember when I went through puberty," Old Man Jenkins said. "It was the hardest hundred years of my life."

"A HUNDRED YEARS!!!!"

"Yeah, that's how long it usually takes for most Zombies. Though, some kids go through it even longer."

"WHAT!!!!"

"Didn't your mom and dad tell you about this stuff?"

"No. . ."

"Man, these modern parents think they know everything, with their homeschoolin' and vegan lunch boxes, and stuff. But they don't even know how to teach a kid the ropes. It figures. . ."

"Sniff. . .sniff. . ."

"But don't worry, Zombie. I know a potion that can help you slow down your growth spurt. Got it from Betsy, a witch I dated once. She made it for me so that my skin would stop clearing up. Yeah, Betsy really liked my rough and scaly zombie skin, especially when it had some big, pus-filled pimples on it. She said it made me look manly."

"Uh. . .Mr. Jenkins, do you still have the potion?"

"I think I have one bottle left in my truck," he said.

Then he jumped into the back of his truck, which was also his house, and came out with two really old and dusty potion bottles."

46

"WEEEHOOO, here they are! Boy, do these bring back memories. Uh. . .let's see. . .which one is it again? . . . Hmm. . ." he said as he sniffed them, while scratching his rough, scaly and pimply head.

"Uh. . .yeah, that's right. Here you go, Zombie," he said as he handed me one.

"Thank you, Mr. Jenkins. Thank you, thank you, thank you!"

"But remember, just take a few drops before you go to bed and you'll be a new Zombie by morning."

"OK, thanks again, Mr. Jenkins!"

Oh man! This is it!

My luck is really turning around.

Now I can pursue my dream of being the most popular kid in school again.

And this time, nothing's gonna stop me!

Monday

I woke up this morning and I was back to normal again.

All thanks to Old Man Jenkin's potion.

So when I got to school, I went back to finish my research.

CLICKETY CLACK, CLICKETY CLACK, CLICKETY CLACK.

Great! Here's that article again. . .

'HOW TO BE A POPULAR ZOMBIE IN 3 EASY STEPS'

OK. So, what's the next thing it says?

BE FRIENDLY

Be friendly. Popular zombies are friendly with pretty much everyone—not only their friends, but also teachers, supervisors, the grocery store clerk, the janitor, parents, the kids at school, and anybody who could use a little happiness in their day.

OK. I can do that.

I just need to be nice to everybody. But man, that could take a long time.

I know! I'll just say hi to everybody I pass in school. That should make me the most popular kid in school by lunchtime.

RRRRRIIIIINNNGGG!!!

Well, there's the bell. This is my chance.

"Hi"

"Hi"

"Hello."

"Hello."

"Howdy."

"Howdy."

"Wassup son?"

"SQUEAK, SQUEAK, SQUEAK?"

"Wassup Brah?"

"SQUEAK, SQUEAK, SQUEAK!"

"SQUEAK, SQUEAK, SQUEAK!"

"LOOK!" I heard somebody yell!

"HAHAHAHA!"

Then the kids started pointing at me and laughing again.

I meant to scratch my head to figure out what was happening, but I missed.

Then I reached for my head and missed again.

For some reason, every time I tried to touch my face, I kept missing.

Then I heard Darius start up.

"Hey, Zombie, your head is so small, you need to use a tea bag for a pillow!" Darius said.

"HAHAHAHA!"

"Hey, Zombie, your head is so small, when you wake up you start singing "Everything is Awesome!" Quentin said.

"HAHAHAHA!"

"Hey, Zombie, your head is so small, you can use a shoelace for a blindfold!" Chad said.

"HAHAHAHA!"

"SQUEAK, SQUEAK, SQUEAK!"

"HAHAHAHA!"

"SQUEAK, SQUEAK, SQUEAK!"

I wanted to say something. But for some reason every time I opened my mouth, I sounded like a mouse in a boys' choir.

So, I ran to the bathroom because I wanted to see what everybody was laughing at.

WHAT THE WHAT THE WHAT?!!!!!

"SQUEAK, SQUEAK, SQUEAK, SQUEAK, SQUEAK!!!"

It's a good thing nobody could understand me because I just said every bad word I could think of.

Then I did my walk of shame all the way to the janitor's closet.

You know, I should probably make myself at home in there.

It is actually kind of cozy. . .

In a janitor's smelly butt kind of way.

Tuesday

Today, I thought I had to go to school looking like somebody put my head in a pencil sharpener.

It's a good thing that Old Man Jenkin's potion wore off.

I was lucky, too, because we have a field trip today.

And in order to get there, I have to ride the school bus with Darius and his minions.

But you know, it's actually supposed to be a pretty cool field trip today.

We're going to the Museum of Nether History.

It's supposed to have all the cool history stuff about the Nether.

Like the history of the Nether Fortress, an exhibit about the lava pits, and some Ghasts are even supposed to do a flyby.

Ooooh, I hope we get to visit the volcano too. That would be so off the hook.

I just want to see it fart. . . just once.

"Hey, Zombie, you're so dumb that you stared at a cup of orange juice because it said concentrate!" Darius said.

"HAHAHAHA!"

Oh, man, here we go again. . .

"Hey, Skelly, you're so ugly, you made an onion cry!"

"HAHAHAHA!"

"Hey, Creepy, you're so clumsy, you tripped over a cordless phone!"

"HAHAHAHA!"

Man, this is what it was like on the bus all the way to the museum.

Now, I would come up with a comeback, but I know my mom and dad wouldn't approve.

Yeah, right.

It's more like whenever I try one of my comebacks, nobody laughs.

Like one time I said, "Oh, yeah? Well your breath smells like boogers."

Yeah. . .nobody laughed.

It's probably because every kid's breath smells like boogers.

RRRRUUUUMMMMBBBBLLLLEEEE!!!!!

All of sudden, I heard that same rumbling sound I heard at Steve's house but much louder. It even shook the school bus.

AAAAAAAAHHHHH!!!

"It's OK, kids, it's just the volcano releasing gas. There's nothing to worry about," Ms. Bones said.

Aw man, I really wanted to see the volcano do that up close.

When we got to the museum, it was awesome.

Our tour guide was a Wither Skeleton named Dr. Patella, and he had a Blaze for an assistant.

They showed us everything.

"Hey, can we see the volcano up close?" I
asked.

"Unfortunately, the volcano tour is closed for
safety reasons," Dr. Patella said.

"Hey, I thought they said it was safe?" one of
the other kids said.

"Uh. . .Yes, it is. We. . .Uh, just don't want any
accidents, you know. But. . .uh. . .move along
kids, this way to the Ghast Flyby exhibition."

I don't know. It sounded kinda fishy to me.

"Hey, guys, is it me or did that Wither
Skeleton sound like he was hiding
something?"

"I. . .sniff. . .don't. . .sniff. . .know. . .sniff,"
Creepy said, still sobbing from the tongue
lashing we got from Darius and his friends.

"What? You don't think the volcano is active, do you?" Skelly asked.

"I don't know. It just seemed like the tour guide was hiding something."

"Hey, guys, look at this," Slimey said, pointing to the sign in front of the Nether Volcano exhibit.

Welcome to the NETHER National Park giant Supervolcano. The lava from this volcano is the source of all the NETHER's famous lava pools, geysers, and hot springs.

The supervolcano erupts about every 600,000 years, and it's been about that long since the last eruption. That means the volcano could erupt any day now, and if it does it'll send a cloud of dust and ash into the sky so big it will blot out the sun for years, along with blowing a 25-mile-wide crater in the

NETHER, destroying every living thing on the planet.

A group of zombie scientists and engineers are currently developing a plan to prevent an eruption by stealing the volcano's lava. Supervolcanoes like the one in the NETHER spend hundreds of years gradually building up heat until they reach a critical point and then they erupt. But outlets like lava pools, geysers and hot springs can bleed out some of that heat, delaying the inevitable eruption.

The scientist's plan is to drill a hole into the side of the volcano and pump out enough lava to prevent it from ever erupting.

Our scientists hope this program will work because, if not, it's only a matter of time before this supervolcano will explode and all life in the Minecraft world will cease to exist.

Thank you for visiting. We hope you enjoyed our tour.

"WHAT THE CRAZY, WHAT?!!!"

"This thing says that the Nether volcano can erupt any day now!"

"But the tour guide said there was nothing to worry about, right, Zombie?" Creepy asked.

"I don't know, but I don't trust him. Wither Skeletons are really sneaky, you know."

"Hey, that's my uncle," Skelly said.

"Oh, sorry."

RRRRUUUUMMMMBBBBLLLLEEEE!!!!!

"Oh man, there it is again!" Slimey said.

We all just looked at each other not knowing what to think.

"Hey, you boys need to get back to the group before you get lost," Dr. Patella said.

"We wouldn't want any of you to have an accident, now would we?"

I sure didn't like the way that Dr. Patella looked at me with those sunken black eye sockets.

It sure does feel like he's hiding something.

Wednesday

Well, things have been pretty quiet the past few days.

No crazy, weird body changes, thank goodness.

My dad told me that during puberty, Minecraft mob kid changes happen in spurts.

And, he said that most of the changes are only temporary until my body ultimately evolves into its final form.

Kinda like a Pixelmon.

But, I don't know if I like that.

It sounds like my looks are going to be based on the luck of the draw.

And that really creeps me out.

Like, what if I turn out to look like some kind of weirdo?

Or what if I turn out to look like some kind of monster?

Or what if I end up looking like this guy?

I mean, I'm sure this guy didn't plan to look that ugly his whole life.

Well, at least the good thing is that I didn't have to worry about any changes these last few days.

But I wish I could say the same about the guys.

Like, Creepy got hit really hard this week.

He's still trying to get used to using his new legs right now.

And Slimey got so big that he can't even fit in school.

But, at least now he can get back at all the kids that make fun at him.

The good thing is that Darius got his fair share of body changes, too.

I thought he was really going to get a taste of his own medicine.

I was even getting my list of insults ready.

69

But then he ended up becoming the best player on our school's basketball team.

And now he's the most popular kid in school.

Figures.

Wednesday – Later that day...

Man, I should've kept my mouth shut.

No, really, I've got hair in my mouth now.

That's because I started growing hair where my lips would normally be.

Yep, it just grew in like a few hours ago.

The only problem is that now people are acting really weird around me.

Like, after school, I bumped into Ms. Bones, my homeroom teacher.

Next thing I know, she started brushing her wig back and doing some weird thing with her eye sockets.

"Hey they're good lookin'" she said.

I didn't know whether to run or hurl.

So I just hurled.

Bad move… I think it made it worse.

And then everybody else started acting weird around me too.

"Excuse me sir, would you like a job?" the principal said.

"Excuse me sir, can you help me with my taxes?" an old lady said.

"Excuse me sir, can you be my daddy?" the kid next door said.

Yeah, it was crazy.

Then my mom and dad took me and Wesley out to dinner at Freddy's Arcade Emporium.

"What do you think you're doing?" the lady clerk said as I jumped into the ball pit.

"Uh….playing?"

"You should be ashamed of yourself!" she said.

"Uh…OK."

I should've known she would be trouble. Especially when she gave my Dad a weird look for paying the PeeWee price for me and Wesley.

When I got home my Dad said that I should probably shave.

He said if my mustache kept growing, it would grow into my ears and eventually take over my head.

He said that happened to my uncle once.

They said he got lost and was never seen again.

Man, I really started to like that mustache too.

Dirk Manly would be so proud.

Thursday

"OK, class, quiet down," Ms. Crabb, our Phys Ed teacher, said. "Today we're going to learn about what happens to a Minecraft mob's body at your age. It seems like a lot of you kids have been going through some changes lately."

Boy, she wasn't kidding.

Our class looked like they just released a Mutant Creatures Mod in Minecraft.

"First, I am going to hand out some questions. Please answer them as best as you can. And don't worry, no one will know it was you."

Then Ms. Crabb passed out a sheet of paper with questions on it.

Here's what some of the questions said:

Do your feet and hands seem to be in different places all the time?

Wait, what?

Have you turned into an eating machine? Like, have you ever woken up one morning and your pillow was gone?

Whoa, I just thought my mom took it. . .

Do you get weird-sized objects growing in strange places on your body? And do those objects ever speak to you from time to time?

What the what?!!!

Do your find that your hair and skin get so greasy that when you high five someone you fall on the floor?

Whoa! I just thought I was clumsy.

Do people hold their noses when they are around you? Or do they remove their noses when they are around you?

Seriously?!! I just thought they didn't like my jokes.

Do your moods change from one minute to the next? Like are you're really mad one minute but then you start crying all of a sudden?

Ugh! I hate these questions!

Sniff. . .but they're so true. . .sniff, sniff.

"OK, class, now turn in your papers," Mrs. Crabb said. "And, remember, these are confidential. So, nobody will know it was you."

I don't know. I have this strange feeling that the teachers get together in the teacher's lounge and just read our papers out loud for laughs.

"OK, class, now going through changes is absolutely normal," Ms. Crabb said, "even though some of the things that happen to you can feel very strange."

"So don't be surprised when you start growing hair where there was none before. . .like your eyeballs."

"And don't be surprised if you start sweating more and start to smell human. Yes, it's disgusting, but you can always use Odor-ant to cover it up."

"And don't be surprised if your body seems to be doing its own thing. Like if parts of your body start to grow and change shape, it just means you're becoming the mob you were meant to be. . . "

". . .Or, it could be the latest Minecraft update, which unfortunately means you're out of luck."

Huh?!!!

"And don't be surprised if your voice starts to change or that you are more clumsy than usual. It's only temporary," she said.

"Most importantly, don't be surprised if you spontaneously grow emo-hair and feel moody all of a sudden. . ."

Hey, was she looking at me?

Hmph! Who cares about this class anyway.

Friday

CLICKETY CLACK, CLICKETY CLACK, CLICKETY CLACK.

All right, where's that article again?

Here it is. . .

'HOW TO BE A POPULAR ZOMBIE IN 3 EASY STEPS'

OK. Now what's the last thing I need to do to achieve middle school stardom?

GET INVOLVED

Joining a club or school activity is another way to broaden your horizons and to meet more people. Find something you're interested in or even just curious about, and try to put yourself in a leadership role.

Being more involved in school activities will help you get recognized; it put's your name out there and helps you get to know more people from different walks of life.

So get more involved, huh?

Now what kind of school activity can a Zombie like me be involved in?

It's got to be something that will make me instantly popular.

I guess that means I probably need to quit the Chess club, Robotics club, and definitely stay away from the World of Warcraft clubs.

Man, I'm gonna miss those.

Suddenly, the clouds parted, and I heard a voice from heaven. . .

"ALL THOSE INTERESTED IN RUNNING FOR STUDENT BODY PRESIDENT MUST SUBMIT THEIR NAMES BY THREE O'CLOCK TODAY AT THE PRINCIPAL'S OFFICE."

Well, it wasn't Mojang, but it definitely felt like somebody up there likes me.

So, I ran to the principal's office and submitted my name to run for school president.

I found out there was only one other person running for school president.

So I thought I had this totally in the bag.

That is, until I read the name of the person I was running against. . .

Figures.

Saturday

"**H**ow am I supposed to beat Darius and become the next eighth grade student body president?"

"I don't know," Slimey said. "But it says here that the election is next week Wednesday. That means you have a few days to get as many votes as you can."

"Yeah, and right now, Darius is the most popular kid in school," Skelly said. "But, you know, I'm kinda surprised Darius is the only one running."

"Yeah, I think he threatened every kid who was running to drop out of the race."

"Well Zombie, your only chance to get the most votes is at the eighth-grade assembly, which is happening in the auditorium right before they vote," Creepy said. "So you need to come up with a seriously killer speech."

"Yeah, like promise them something that every kid wants. . .like no more homework. . . or cancel all gym classes," Skelly said.

"Or, you could promise them that every bully in school will have to pay a million dollars to every kid they ever tormented in school. . .especially those they gave wedgies to," Creepy said stroking his behind.

"Or you could do arm farts. Those'll get you a lot of votes," Slimey said.

You know, the guys were right.

Something told me that if I was going to be student president that I needed to give the kids at school something so awesome, they would have to make me president.

But what could it be?

What could it be?

Sunday

I went to go visit Steve today to see what he was up to.

"Hey, Zombie. Wassup, brah?"

"What in the world is that?" I asked, pointing to the huge mountain that was behind his house.

"Man, I don't know. All I know is that I went to visit Glenda the witch to get some supplies, and when I got back there it was."

There was also a group of people in white coats setting up equipment at the bottom of the mountain.

"Hey, I know that guy," I said, pointing at the Wither Skeleton in the suit. "He was one of the tour guides at the Nether museum."

"Dude, we should go find out what's up," Steve said.

So we went up to the group of about ten people who were setting up equipment.

"Hey, mister, why are you guys setting up in my backyard?" Steve asked.

"Uh. . . no important reason. We're just taking soil samples to make sure that the. . .um. . .the environment is nice and healthy to grow flowers here."

I was getting that feeling again. Like that this guy was hiding something.

"Hey, aren't you Skelly's uncle, Dr. Patella?" I asked.

"Yes, yes, I am."

"Skelly said that you're part of the research team that's studying the Nether volcano," I said. "I guess you're checking to see if the volcano is going to erupt, right?"

I was trying to be sneaky and get as much information as I could.

"Oh no, no, no, no, no. . . ahem. I'm actually just here. . . uh. . .checking to see if the cactuses are growing like they should. But. . . excuse me, I have to go!" he said as he scurried away like a rat.

"I don't know, man. Something tells me that there's a lot more going on than he's letting on."

Then Steve and I both looked at each other. . .

"Dun, Dun, Duuuunnn!"

"PFFFFFFFTTTTT!!!"

Then we just broke out laughing.

"Hey, Zombie, come check this out," Steve said as we walked back to his house.

Inside his house was a brewing stand with a few potions brewing.

"What's all that for?" I asked.

"Well, I'm trying to come up with a potion that can cure every kid of ever having to go through puberty. And if it works, I'll be rich!"

"Well, does it work?"

"I don't know. But I need somebody to try it on," Steve said while rubbing his hands and looking at me with a really weird smile on his face.

"No way, no way, no way!" I said. "You remember what happened last time. Not only did I almost lose all my street cred, I almost got eaten by a killer rabbit on the way home."

"All right. I guess I could test it on some of the villagers around here. It's not like anybody can hear their screams anyway," he said.

Then we both looked at each other. . .

"Dun, Dun, Duuuunnn!"

"PFFFFFFFTTTTT!!!"

Monday

I spent the entire day giving out flyers to get more votes for the school election.

'ZOMBIE FOR PRESIDENT' is what it said. 'VOTE FOR ME AND GET A FREE A+ IN EVERY CLASS.'

The kids seemed to really like it.

But, I really think it was because of my arm farts. Those always attract a crowd.

Though, I was wondering how I was going deliver on my campaign promises, and get every kid a FREE A+ in every class.

But I didn't have time to think about the details right now.

I just needed to get as many votes as possible.

"ZOMBIE FOR PRESIDENT!"

"VOTE FOR ME AND GET A FREE A+ IN EVERY CLASS!"

PFFPTT! PFFPTT! PFFPTT!

"ZOMBIE FOR PRESIDENT!"

"VOTE FOR ME AND GET A FREE A+ IN EVERY CLASS!"

PFFPTT! PFFPTT! PFFPTT!

Tuesday

"**H**ey, Zombie, all the kids in school are talking about you!" Slimey said.

"Yeah, it looks like you just might win the election after all," Creepy said.

"You just have to clinch it with your speech tomorrow, and you got this in the bag," Skelly said.

Oh, man, I can imagine it now. . .

ZACK ZOMBIE HAS BEEN ELECTED PRESIDENT OF THE MINECRAFT MOB MIDDLE SCHOOL!

RAAAAAAAAAHHHHHH!!!

IN A STUNNING LANDSLIDE UPSET, THIS ALL-AROUND GREAT GUY HAS BECOME THE MOST POPULAR KID EVER IN ALL OF MOB MIDDLE SCHOOL HISTORY!

RAAAAAAAAAHHHHHH!!!

. . .AND HIS ARM FARTS ARE LEGENDARY!

RAAAAAAAAAHHHHHH!!!

"Hey, Zombie, what are you looking up at?"
Skelly asked.

"Nuthin'. I'm good. . .I'm good."

RRRRUUUUMMMMMBBBBLLLLEEEE!!!!!

Suddenly, the ground started to shake again.
But this time we felt it in school!

"What was that?!!!" Slimey asked.

"I don't know, but I think it was the volcano,"
I said.

"The volcano?!!!!" Skelly blurted.

"HSSSSSSSSSS!" was all Creepy had to say.

"Yeah, Steve said it passes gas like that once
in a while. But, this is weird. I never felt it in
school before."

Oh, man, I hope that thing doesn't ruin the election.

This is like my only chance to be the most popular kid in school, and I can't let anything stop me right now.

But how in the world am I supposed to stop a volcano?

Wednesday

"So vote for me because I'm cool, and Zombie's a fool," Darius yelled. "Peace out!"

Bump! SKRREEEECH!

"OK, everyone. Let's give a round of applause for Darius Flenderman for that. . .uh. . .very colorful speech," the principal said.

Clap, clap, clap, yawn, clap.

"And now we will take a five-minute break, and after that we will have Zack Zombie come up and tell us why he should be president of the eighth-grade student body," the principal said. "And please no mic dropping. . .that equipment is expensive."

Well, this is it.

I got my speech ready, and I practiced my secret clinch move that I'm going to pull out to seal the deal!

The good thing is that besides a few pimples that have disappeared from my forehead, it seems like my body is keeping it together.

I haven't heard any rumbling either, so I don't think I have to worry about any volcanos.

Man, what was I thinking. . .That volcano hasn't erupted in like 600,000 years. There's no way that thing is gonna mess with me now.

Anyway, now is my turn to shine!

"Everyone, please give a warm welcome to Zack Zombie."

Clap, clap, yawn, clap, clap.

"Uh. . .Hi, everybody. My name is Zack Zombie, and I'm. . .um, running for school president."

Cricket, cricket. Cricket.

"Uh. . .I wanted to start by telling you why you should make me president. You should make me president because I promise to. . .uh. . .I promise to get rid of homework forever!"

"Yeah!" Clap, clap, clap, clap!

"I promise to. . .make school only one hour every day!"

"Yeah, Zombie! Woohoo!" Clap, clap, clap, clap!

"I promise to make every teacher eat the lunchroom food!"

"YEEEAAAHHHHH!!!!"

"I promise to make all bullies pay one million dollars to every kid they ever messed with!"

WOOOHHOOOO!!!!

"Especially those they gave wedgies to!"

"WAY TO GO ZOMBIE!" Creepy yelled. CLAP, CLAP, CLAP, CLAP!!!!

"I promise to lock all the mean girls in the janitor's closet!"

YEAH!!! RIGHT ON ZOMBIE!!!

"And I promise to. . .I promise to. . ."

". . .Give every kid a free A+ just for showing up to school!"

RAAAAAAAAAAAHHHHH!!!!

By this time, the crowd was going wild.

I had them eating out of my hand.

All the kids were on their feet yelling and screaming in joy.

I was really getting into it to. I felt a rush go through my body.

"AND IF YOU MAKE ME PRESIDENT TODAY, I PROMISE TO. . . GRRRAAWWWWLLLLLAAAWWAGGG!"

Suddenly, everything went quiet.

"I SAID, I PROMISE TO. . . RRAAWWKKGGWWHHOOMMOORRGG!!"

What the what?!!!

"LOOOOOOK!" somebody yelled.

Suddenly, all the kids were looking up at me with terror on their faces.

I didn't know what to do, so I just pulled out my secret clinch move. . .

PFFPTT!

PFFPTT!

PFFPTT!

PFFPTT!

"AAAAAAAAAAAHHHH!!!!!!"

Then all the kids just started screaming and yelling and running all over the auditorium.

I tried to finish my speech, but the more I tried to talk, the crazier things got.

GRRRAAWWWWLLLLLAAAWWAGGG!

"AAAAAAAAAAAHHHH!!!!!!"

Then, suddenly, Darius and his minions jumped in.

"Hey, Zombie, you're so ugly, you went to a haunted house and left with a job application!" Darius said.

Then everyone started laughing at me.

"HAHAHAHA!"

"Hey, Zombie, you're so ugly you have to trick or treat over the phone!" Quentin said.

"HAHAHAHA!"

"Hey, Zombie, you're so ugly, that when you were born, instead of slapping you, the doctor slapped your mother!" Chad said.

"HAHAHAHA!"

Then everybody was in an uproar, pointing fingers and laughing at me.

I couldn't take it anymore, so I just ran to the janitor's closet.

Except this time, I was too big to fit. So I just ran home.

All the kids were running behind me, yelling insults at me, and I think carrying pitchforks.

When I finally got home, I couldn't fit through the front door either, so my mom opened the garage door and brought me a blanket.

105

Then I just laid there and cried myself to sleep. . .

Again.

Thursday

When I woke up today, I breathed a sigh of relief because I knew my body changes were only temporary.

"SIGH. . .
GRRRAAWWWWLLLLLAAAWWAGGG!"

What the what?!!!!

"GRRRAAWWWWLLLLLAAAWWAGGG!"

Then I grabbed the car side mirror so I could look at myself. But it broke off.

I tried looking at myself, but my head was so big that I couldn't see my whole face.

Then I called my mom.

"GRRRAAWWWWLLLLLAAAWWAGGG!"

I kept calling her, but for some reason she didn't come.

"GRRRAAWWWWLLLLLAAAWWAGGG!"

Then I decided to go to the only person I knew who could help me.

"Whoa, Zombie! Is that you?"

"GRRRAAWWWWLLLLLAAAWWAGGG!"

"Dude, what happened?" Steve asked.

"GRRRAAWWWWLLLLLAAAWWAGGG!"

"What? You were about to win the election and then you went through some crazy mutant metamorphosis?"

"GRRRAAWWWWLLLLLAAAWWAGGG!"

"And then Darius and his friends started making fun of you. . ."

"GRRRAAWWWWLLLLLAAAWWAGGG!"

". . .And then the whole school was pointing fingers and laughing at you?"

"GRRR. . .?"

"Naw, I don't know what in the world you're saying," Steve said. "The guys just came by last night and told me everything that happened."

Then I just broke down crying.

"GRRRAAWWWWLLLLLAAAWWAGGG! Sniff. . .sniff. . ."

"So, I guess you're probably ready to try my new 'PU-BE-GONE' potion?"

"GRRR. . .?"

"Yeah, I'm still working on the name. But, I think it's ready. And you can be the first to try it."

I must be crazy. But, what have I got to lose. I didn't have anywhere else to turn.

Plus, nothing could be worse than this.

I mean like, is this what I'm supposed to look like for the rest of my life?

No way!

"GRRRAAWWWWLLLLLAAAWWAGGG!"

"All right, let's do this!" Steve said as he picked up a potion bottle from the brewing stand.

"So, you need to drink the whole thing this time. Every drop," he said as he strapped me to a table.

110

"GRRR. . .?"

"Oh no. The straps are just as a precaution.
Heh, heh. . .Here you go, drink up."

Gulp, gulp, gulp, gulp, gulp!

The potion didn't taste too bad. Kinda tasted
like a mix of a Z-Monster and a 4-Hour
Energy mixed together. . .with a pumkin twist.

I didn't really feel anything.

Nothing at all. . .

Not even a little bit. . .

Not even. . .

GLECH!

GLUB!

GLUG!

GLACK!

GLOF!

GLOOB!

GLAMACK!

BOOOOOOOOOMMMMM!!!!

Next thing I know, I crashed right through the roof of Steve's house!

"What's happening to me?!!!!!"

"Uh. . .don't worry, buddy, this might be just a side effect," Steve said.

I just kept growing and growing and growing and growing.

Until, finally, it stopped.

"WAAAAAAAAAHHHHHH!!!!!"

"Don't cry, man!" Steve yelled. "Look at the bright side. Now you're all evened out."

"WAAAAAAAAAHHHHHH!!!!!"

I knew I couldn't go back to school looking like this.

I can't even face my mom and dad like this either.

I mean, everybody made fun of me before. Now they're really going to laugh at me.

That's why I just need to run away.

Forever!

113

Friday

So I ran away to live in the forest biome by myself.

Man, I already miss my mom and dad and all my friends.

But I might as well get used to being alone.

Nobody is going to want to be around a monster like me.

Just look at me. . .Sniff.

Trying to find a place to sleep when you're this size is really hard, though.

Not to mention finding a place to poop.

It's a good thing there are a lot of really big bushes in Minecraft.

To sleep on, I mean.

The hard part was finding a place to hide when the sun came up.

Lucky for me, I found a giant redwood tree to hide under.

Took me a while to find it, though. . .

"Hey, dude."

"Who's that?"

"It's me, Steve."

"Where?" I asked as I looked around.

"Down here."

"Oh, yeah, sorry."

"How you doing, buddy? You holding up all right?" Steve asked.

"No, I'm a total loser. Look at me. I'm a monster and nobody wants me!"

"Yeah, you are big. . .and ugly too."

"Huh?"

"Well, that is what you want me to say, right?" Steve said.

"No, but I know it's true."

RRRRUUUUMMMMBBBBLLLLEEEE!!!!!

"Well, right now, I think the whole town could use a monster to help us with a really big problem," Steve said.

"Huh?"

RRRRUUUUMMMMBBBBLLLLEEEE!!!!!

"You hear that? That's the volcano. And they said on the news today that the scientists have been working on stopping the volcano for months. And they've done everything they could, but they can't stop it. It's going to blow. . .today!"

"WHAT?!!!!"

"And if it does blow, that's going to be the end of Minecraft as we know it. That means no more Mom, no more Dad. No more friends. No more school. . .no more Steve."

"SERIOUSLY?"

"And the only way to stop it is to plug up that hole on the giant mountain next to my house," Steve said. "But there's nobody around big enough or strong enough to do it."

"REALLY?"

"Yep. So, I don't know about you, buddy, but if I'm gonna go, I want to go sitting next to my brother," Steve said. "So move on over and give me a little room, will ya?"

I moved over a little and Steve sat next to me.

So we just sat there for a few minutes.

"Uh. . .hey, Steve."

"Yeah, Zombie."

"I'm kinda big, right?"

"Yeah."

"And I'm really strong."

"Yeah, what about it?"

"I could probably plug up that hole, right?"

"Probably, but a loser couldn't do it. Only a really brave kid, who finally realized that all the changes he's being going through just made him an even more special kid than he already was. . .so special, in fact, that he's the only one in the whole world who can save us all today," Steve said.

"Really?"

"Yup. That special kid, he could do it," Steve said. "If only he was around to help us right now. . .at this moment. . .when we need him most. . .when his buddy Steve is in trouble. . ."

Then we just sat there for a few more minutes.

"Uh, hey, Steve."

"Yeah, buddy?"

"Let's do this!"

"My man!"

120

Saturday

BOOOOOOOOOMMMMM!!!!!!

By time we got back to Steve's house, it was too late.

The volcano exploded, and a huge cloud of ash filled the sky.

We ran into Dr. Patella when we got there.

"Is it too late?" I asked Dr. Patella.

"No, there is still time. That was just the first explosion. The really big one that is going to wipe us all out is coming. Zombie, we need you to find something to plug up that volcano fast!"

"What can I do?" Steve asked.

"Help me evacuate the town," Dr. Patella said. "That ash cloud is going to make it really hard for everybody in town to breathe."

As I looked around, I couldn't recognize anything. The whole town was covered in ash.

"Hey, Zombie, you can do this!" Steve yelled. "And remember, you can always do that nasty thing that you do!"

Then he gave me a thumbs up and ran off to help evacuate the town.

So, I ran all the way to the volcano.

By now, the ash cloud was so thick that I could hardly see anything.

But as I felt around, I felt the top of the volcano, and it was red hot with lava.

I looked around for a big boulder to plug it up with, but I couldn't find one.

Suddenly. . .

RRRUUUUUUUUUMMMMBBBBLLLLLEEE!!!!

I could tell that the rumbling sound was even stronger than ever before.

This must be the big one, I thought.

Then I remembered what Steve said, 'You could always do that nasty thing that you do!'

So I pulled up my shirt, reached over and. . .

123

"POP!"

And then I slammed it on top of the volcano with all my strength.

BAAAMMM!

RRRRUUUUMMMMBBBBLLLLEEEE!!!!!

RRRRUUUUMMMMBBBBLLLLEEEE!!!!!

RRRRUUUUUUUUUUUUUMMMMMMMM-
MMBBBBBBBBBBLLLLEEEE!!!!!

FIZZZZZZZZZ!

Then instead of blowing up, the volcano just fizzled out.

"YEEEEAAAHHHHHH!!!!!!!!" I heard everybody in town yelling.

"You did it!" Steve and Dr. Patella said.

124

"Dr. Patella, is there anything else I could do?" I asked.

"No, Zombie, that was perfect. The volcano just found another way to release the pressure. Unfortunately, the Nether is never going to be the same again. But at least you saved all of Minecraft."

Then everybody in the whole village started cheering again.

RAAAAAAAAAAAHHHHH!!!!

Then I clapped my hands together as hard as I could, and the entire cloud of ash just disappeared.

RAAAAAAAAAAAHHHHH!!!!

It seemed like everything I did got the crowd going.

125

So, then I did what every green-blooded hero would do in this situation. . .

"Boomdiyadda, Boomdiyadda, Boomdiyadda, Boomdiyadda.

I love the mountains.

I love the clear blue skies.

I love big bridges.

I love when wolves run by.

I love the whole world.

And all explosive sounds.

"Boomdiyadda, Boomdiyadda, Boomdiyadda, Boomdiyadda.

I love some redstone.

I love my zombie friends.

I love hot laba. . .

Hob lava. . .

Hob laba. . ."

Oh boy. . .

Sunday

Well, I woke up today and I'm back to normal.

I'm my normal size, and my lips are OK too.

It seems that Dr. Patella has also been working on an experimental potion for treating puberty in Minecraft Mobs too.

He calls it 'Pu-Liberty.'

It should be on shelves by Christmas.

And man, does it work wonders.

But you know, now that I think about it, unless I had gone through puberty I probably wouldn't have been able to stop the volcano.

Then all the people I care about wouldn't be around anymore.

So I guess, even though it was a little rough going through all those weird body changes, it really helped me do something special.

. . .Something that no one else could do.

And I guess it made me an even more special version of who I am.

Oh, man. . .I'm starting to sound like my parents.

Blech!

Well, at least the good thing is, after saving the town, now I'm the most popular kid in school.

Not even Darius can get away with calling me names anymore.

"Hey, Zombie, you're so dumb, you tried to save a fish from drowning!" Darius said.

"Hey, Darius, you're so ugly that One Direction went the other way!" Brad said.

"HAHAHAHA!"

"Hey, Darius, you're so ugly you turned Medusa into stone!" Velma said.

"HAHAHAHA!"

"Hey, Darius, you're so ugly, you scare blind kids away!" Braden said.

"HAHAHAHA!"

Yeah, I've got so many fans now, they totally got my back.

So, I went to go see Steve today to see how he was doing.

"Hey, Steve."

"Hey, Zombie. What's crackin'?"

"Uh, nothing much, just the usual. How you doin'?"

"Good, I'm just trying to decide what to do with that big mountain behind my house."

Then I looked up and saw the huge mountain with what looked like a big green avocado on top of it.

"At least I don't have to see you do that nasty thing you do anymore," Steve said.

"Oh, you mean this?"

"POP!"

"Dude, that is wrong on so many levels. How'd you grow back your outie, anyway? I thought since you left yours on top of the mountain, I wouldn't ever have to see it again."

"Well, you know. . .

. . .Puberty."

The End

Find out What
Happens Next in. . .

Diary of a Minecraft Zombie Book 15
"Attack of the Gnomes"

Please Leave Us a Review

Please support us by leaving a review.
The more reviews we get, the more
books we will write!

And if you really liked this book,
please tell a friend.

I'm sure they will be happy you told
them about it.

Check Out Our Other Books from Zack Zombie Publishing

The Diary of a Minecraft Zombie Book Series

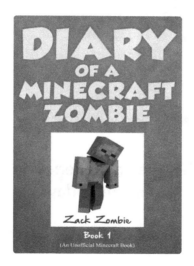

Get The Entire Series on Amazon Today!

The Ultimate Minecraft Comic Book Series

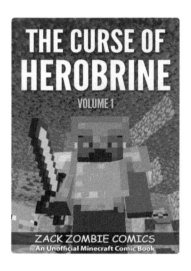

Get the Entire Series on Amazon Today!

Herobrine's Wacky Adventures

Get The Entire Series on Amazon Today!

The Mobbit

An Unexpected Minecraft Journey

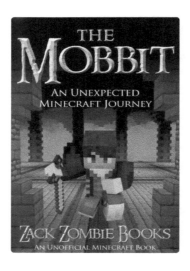

Get The Entire Series On Amazon Today!

Minecraft
Galaxy Wars

Get The Entire Series on
Amazon Today!

Ultimate Minecraft Secrets:

An Unofficial Guide to Minecraft Tips, Tricks and Hints to Help You Master Minecraft

Get Your Copy on Amazon Today!